I0456933

A Knife in the Heart

GREAT STORIES: HIGH BEGINNER

JOHN MCRAE

WAYZGOOSE PRESS

CONTENTS

Before You Read   v

Chapter 1   1
Chapter 2   4
Chapter 3   8
Chapter 4   10
Chapter 5   13
Chapter 6   17
Chapter 7   20
Chapter 8   23
Chapter 9   27

After You Read   29
About the Publisher   33

BEFORE YOU READ

VOCABULARY

Here are some important words in this story. Read the definitions and example sentences. If you don't feel that you understand the word completely, check a bilingual dictionary.

- **client**: a person who hires a professional to do a job; a customer. *The lawyer got a new client this week.*
- **crime**: activities that are against the law. *Stealing is a crime.* A common verb with *crime* is *commit*: *She committed a crime.*
- **editor**: In this story, the editor of a newspaper is the manager of the newspaper. The editor decides what stories will be published in the

newspaper, and also decides which reporter will write about each story. *The editor asked the journalist to write a story about a famous actress.*

- **journalist**: A person who writes news stories. At the time of this story, a journalist worked for a printed paper newspaper. *The journalist worked until 10:00 pm to finish writing the story.*

- **justice**: This is a difficult idea to explain in a few words. It means being right—not just right about facts, but right in a moral sense. This is a good word to check in a bilingual dictionary. *Justice is more important to me than money.*

- **killer**: A person who kills. Another common word for this is "murderer." *When I was reading the story, I couldn't guess who the killer was!*

- **lawyer**: A person who studies the law. In detective stories, a lawyer is often the person who tries to defend a person that people believe committed a crime. *I didn't commit a crime! I'm going to hire a lawyer to help me.*

- **murder**: The killing of a person by another person. *That death was not an accident. It was murder!*

- **trap**: A situation where a person can be tricked or deceived. The situation seems safe, but it is not. Because someone believes the situation is safe, they enter into danger. *Don't click that link! It's not a real website—it's a trap!*

- **victim:** A person who is affected by a crime: the person who is robbed, or hurt, or killed. *Do you know the victim's name?*

CULTURE NOTES

Hollywood 1930-1949

The 1930s and 1940s are called the "golden age" of Hollywood. Major studios produced movies and created movie stars. In fact, more than 7,500 movies were made between 1930 and 1945, and more than 80 million people watched at least one movie a week! Movie stars became famous, and people who wanted to act in movies moved to Los Angeles to find jobs.

The art deco movement in fashion and design was still popular. Today, when we think of 1930s Hollywood—the period in this book—we think of movies, glamour, and fashion.

Art deco style

Amateur detective

The 1930s-1940s was a time when detective stories were popular—a crime was committed, and the detective used clues to solve the mystery (Who stole the necklace? Who killed the secretary? Who robbed the bank?). Some detectives were ***professional***—a police officer, for example, or a person who was a full-time detective as their job. Sherlock Holmes is a perfect example of a professional detective.

In stories, the ***amateur detective*** was also popular. An amateur is the opposite of a professional—they are not paid for what they do. It is a hobby or an interest, not a full-time job. The amateur detective in popular stories was a person who learned about a crime by accident, and decided to solve that crime because they were curious, because they knew the victim, or because they wanted the criminal to pay for their crime. Amateur detectives in stories didn't care about money—they cared about justice.

CHAPTER

ONE

WEDNESDAY, MARCH 20, 1940, 1:00 P.M.

It was just another Los Angeles party, Nick wrote in his notebook. *Beautiful women, loud music—but then, at the end of the party, a girl with a knife in her back.*

He looked around the room. Some policemen and detectives were taking photographs.

"Move on," one of the policemen said to Nick.

"But I'm taking notes for a story," said Nick.

"Be quick about it, then," said the policeman. "And then get out."

Nick was a journalist in Los Angeles. He wrote about the dark side of life in the city. There were a lot of actors and actresses trying to find work in Hollywood, the city of dreams just up the road. Was this girl with the knife in her back one of these out-of-work movie people?

Nick went towards the girl's dead body.

"Don't touch anything, mister," said the policeman.

"I just want to look at her," said Nick.

She was tall, blonde, and very pretty. Nick liked tall, blonde, pretty girls. But not one with a knife in her back. That was ugly, violent, and horrible. There were so many murders in this city. *And no justice*, Nick thought. The police never found the killers in most murder cases. *Will they find this one?* he asked himself.

"Who was she?" Nick turned to the detective.

"How do I know?" the detective answered. "Just a girl. She went to a lot of parties. She knew a lot of men. It's the same old story with a lot of girls in the big, bad city of L.A." The detective smiled.

There's nothing to smile about, Nick thought. He looked at the girl again. There was something familiar about her. Did he know her?

He looked at her more closely. Then he saw the terrible scars on her wrist. His heart stopped for a moment. *Can it be...? Is this...? No, it's not possible!* He looked at her other arm—the same scars on the wrist.

"Oh, my God!" he said. He felt sick.

"Hey, these scars will help to tell us who she was," the detective said.

"I think I know who she was."

"Do you? Who was she, then?" asked the detective.

"Her name was Ann Hammond."

"Do you think this place is hers? It looks too good for a girl like her. She was just a good-time girl. Do you think one of her men friends kept her here?"

"She was *not* just a good-time girl," Nick said. He wanted to defend her now that she was dead.

"Killed about ten hours ago," another of the detectives said, after looking at the body carefully.

"At about three in the morning. What a party!"

Nick wanted to know who else was at the party. But first he wanted to touch Ann again, for the last time. He touched her long, blonde hair. *It wasn't blonde when we were together*, he remembered.

The blonde hair came away in his hand. It was not real. It was a wig. Under the wig, Nick saw the Ann he knew. Suddenly she looked very lost, though still very beautiful. At that moment, Nick knew what to do. "I'm going to find her killer," he said.

"Forget her," said the first detective. "She's just another nobody. No good to anyone."

But Nick had a sense of justice—and he had reasons of his own for wanting to find Ann's killer.

"You can forget her if you want," he said to the detective. "But I'm going to find her killer."

CHAPTER
TWO

WEDNESDAY 3:30 P.M.

"How do you know this Ann Hammond?"

Nick did not reply. A good journalist doesn't tell everything he knows—not even to the editor of the newspaper. And Nick's editor was angry.

"How do you know her?" the editor repeated. "If you don't tell me, I'll take you off the story."

"No, boss," said Nick. "Don't do that. I'm the man for the job. I know the situation, and I knew the victim. So I'll be able to make a good story out of it. Give me a couple of days."

'And you don't want to tell me anything before then?"

"That's right. Two days—that's all," said Nick.

The editor was still angry. But he knew Nick was a good journalist. And a good story is important for the newspaper. He waited, thinking.

After a while, the editor spoke. "OK, you win."

"Thanks, boss," said Nick.

"Two days. No more," the editor said. "Friday."

"No problem," said Nick. As he left, he heard the editor's phone ringing.

Five minutes later, the editor called him back to the office. "Problem over. The police arrested the killer half an hour ago."

"Who was it?"

"A waiter. He was at the party. He killed her for money. Something like that."

"I don't believe that," Nick said. "She..."

"Forget it," the editor said, almost angry again. "There's no story. It's over.'

Why was the editor so angry? *He's scared*, Nick thought. *Someone told him to take me off this story. Someone important. But who?*

But Nick only said, "OK, boss. If you say so, it's over. No story." And he left the editor's office.

He was sure the waiter was not the killer. Ann didn't have any money. There was a big story here. And he wanted to find that story to find the real killer. For Ann. For her memory.

Nick was certain that the waiter was in jail for something he did not do. Nick wanted justice for Ann, and now he wanted justice for the waiter too.

Nick went to see the waiter's lawyer. The lawyer had an office in a dirty part of town. He wore dark glasses all the time, even in his office at half past five. He smoked all the time, too. His name was J. T. Morgan. Nick didn't like him.

"I want to help your waiter. I know he's innocent. Tell me his side of the story, Mr. Morgan."

"Call me J.T.," said the lawyer. "The man in jail is Johnny Wong. He works in a Chinese restaurant in the same apartment block where the woman died."

"Why was he in the apartment?" Nick asked.

"They called for food for the party. He took it up to them," the lawyer said. "Three complete meals."

"Only three? For a party? That's important," said Nick.

"You never know. Maybe not everyone was hungry," said J.T.

"Did Johnny Wong see all the people there?" Nick asked.

"He saw six or seven women, he told the police. Women who go to a lot of parties like that."

"How many men?" Nick asked.

"Four," said the lawyer. "A fat man, a thin man, an old man, and a very good-looking man, an actor."

Nick was suddenly more interested. "Who was the actor?"

"Blade Raines. You've seen him in movies. Small parts. He's no big star. But he thinks he is."

"Well, that's a help. I'll start with him. Thanks, Mr. Morgan," said Nick, and started to leave.

"J.T.," said J.T.

As Nick was leaving, the lawyer asked him, "Why are you helping my client? What's in it for you?"

"I'm not helping Johnny Wong," Nick replied. 'I'm doing this for Ann Hammond. Don't ask why. That's another story."

CHAPTER
THREE

FLASHBACK: MARCH 1934

Another story. Another world. Six years ago.

Nick went slowly up the stairs to the fourth floor. There was no elevator. There were bad smells on the stairs. It was that kind of apartment block.

He found number 409—but there was no one there. The old lady who lived there died last week. She left a dog. It cried for a week. This was the story,

"Not much of a story," Nick said to the editor.

"You're young. You do any story I tell you to do," said the editor.

So Nick went next door, to number 408, to get a story about the old lady's dog.

But it was a young lady who opened the door. The kind of girl Nick liked—tall and very pretty, with short, dark hair.

"Who are you? What do you want?" she asked nervously.

"I want to put your name in the papers," said Nick.

"Are you kidding?"

"Tell me about the old lady next door and her dog. That way, your name will be in the papers," he told her.

They went to a bar, had coffee, and talked. She told him all about the dog and the old lady. Still not much of a story.

"Thanks a lot," Nick said, and stood up.

"Is that it?" she asked. "Is that all?"

"That's all," he said.

"But you don't know my name. How will I be in the paper if you don't know my name?"

Nick smiled—she wasn't stupid, this girl. Pretty, too. "What are you doing tonight?" he asked.

"Me? Oh, nothing," she replied.

"You want to come for a drink with me." It wasn't a question really.

"Oh," said the girl. "OK."

"See you later, then, Miss ..."

"Hammond," she said. "Ann Hammond."

WEDNESDAY 11:55 P.M.

It was easy to find a photo of Blade Raines. That kind of actor is always in the papers—at the first night of a movie, at a club, in a restaurant.

Nick was in the office. There weren't many people there—just the printers with the morning edition of the paper and a few journalists like Nick, working on their stories.

Nick found a good photo of Blade taken at Christmas —just three months ago. "Blade Raines, the young star, at a Christmas party at Lola's night club" said the photo caption.

Young! thought Nick. *If he's young, I'm a baby. He's forty at least!*

There was another man in the photo with Blade

Raines. He was fat and oily. He looked dangerous, like a gangster.

What's the 'young star' doing with a man like that? thought Nick. He took the picture from the paper. *Midnight,* he said to himself. *That's the best time to go to a club like Lola's.*

An hour later, Nick was talking to Lola, the owner of the club. She was elegant and sexy, and held her cigarette in a long black holder.

"Yes, I know Blade Raines," she said. "I know lots of people."

They were in her office at the club. On the wall of the club there was a large mirror. But in the office, this mirror was a window to see into the club.

In the club, people were dancing, drinking, smoking, having a good time. In the office, it was quiet. Lola was looking at Nick.

"What do you want from me?" she asked.

He showed her two photos. One was of Ann, in the summer of 1934. The other was of Blade Raines and the fat man.

Lola looked at the first one. She did not say anything.

"This woman died last night," Nick said. He watched Lola's face carefully. It didn't change.

"People die," said Lola.

"She died with a knife in her back."

"It's a big, bad world," said Lola.

"You knew her," said Nick.

"Maybe. I know —"

"Yes—you know a lot of people. Well, what about him?" Nick pointed to the fat man in the other photo.

"Look, mister. I don't know what you want..."

"Who's the fat man? Just tell me that."

Lola took her long cigarette holder from her bright, red lips. Her face was serious. "You're a nice guy," she said. "You don't want to know a man like that. Stay away from him."

"What's his name?"

"Everyone calls him Rico," she said.

"What does he do?"

"I don't know. This and that. Buying, selling ... That kind of thing."

Lola knew a lot more, Nick thought. But she didn't want to tell him. "She's scared, like the editor. There's someone big, someone important, behind all this."

Suddenly the phone rang. Lola answered it.

"Hello? ... Not now ... No, not here ... I can't ... OK, where are you? I'll be there in ten minutes."

Lola went to the door. "I'm going. You stay here in the club. Have a good time. Don't think about men like Rico."

Nick stopped her. "Before you go," he said, "tell me one thing. Who do you think killed Ann Hammond?"

"Men." Lola laughed. "It's always men. It's a man's world. Men killed your darling Ann."

CHAPTER

FIVE

THURSDAY 1:15 A.M.

Lola left the club. Nick waited at the bar for a minute or two, and then he followed Lola outside. He saw her car disappear fast down the empty street.

I know where she's going! he thought suddenly.

It wasn't easy to follow her. Nick didn't want Lola to see his car. But soon they were near the place.

"Yes, I was right," said Nick to himself. They were near the house where the party was—where Ann's body was found. He parked his car and walked to the house. Lola's car was outside.

Nick waited around the corner from the main door. After a few minutes. Lola came out with two men. The men were carrying some boxes from the house.

"Go around the back," said one of the men, "while I put these in the car."

One man put the boxes in Lola's car, while she walked towards Nick with the other man.

Nick moved fast. He went around the back of the building and found an open space, like a small garden. There was a fire burning there, and another man was standing there—a fat man. Was it Rico?

Lola and the other man were coming closer behind Nick. The fat man was in front of him. Nick moved quickly behind the garden wall.

"Where have you been?" the fat man shouted.

Nick stayed very still.

Then Lola spoke. "This journalist guy came to the club," she said. "He had a photo of Ann."

"Put that on the fire," said the fat man to the other man.

Nick looked over the wall. The other man was putting lots of papers—letters, notebooks, documents—on the fire.

"And he knew about Blade," said Lola.

The second man arrived, carrying two more boxes. Lola took one and moved to the fire.

"Wait! Don't put that on the fire," said the fat man.

The other man dropped the box he was carrying. A bag of white powder fell out and burst open on the ground.

"You fool!"

"Sorry, Rico. It was an accident," said the man.

He got down on his knees and tried to clean the powder up.

Rico! thought Nick. *So it **is** him.*

The man called Rico spoke again. "Find Blade Raines before that journalist guy finds him," he said. "Burn all the evidence. And get the snow away from here."

Snow! The gangsters' name for cocaine! Nick thought. *That's the big story.*

Just then, he heard another car arrive. A tall, thin man got out of the car. He was very angry—but it was his uniform that Nick noticed, with surprise. He recognized the man. This was someone important—the chief of the Los Angeles police.

"You're nothing but a stupid, fat fool," shouted the police chief. Nick heard the sound of a hand hitting someone.

"Don't hit me!" cried Rico. The chief hit him again.

"My men were in this house, investigating that woman's murder. With all this stuff in the house—the snow, the lists of names, everything." Another hitting sound, and the Police Chief went on: "Can you imagine? A police chief who tells his men to leave the place? *Not* to investigate? Can you believe that? You made me look like a fool!"

"I'm sorry, boss," cried Rico. "Just don't hit me any more."

"Get away from here. Lola," the police chief said, "take all the stuff and get out."

Lola left without saying a word.

"Now, you fat fool—what happened last night? Who killed this woman Ann Hammond?"

"I don't know, boss," Rico replied. "We had a party

here—we often have parties here. Ann was talking to Blade Raines. He was waiting for Doc Mansfield. When Blade got his stuff, he left the party. Ann went with him."

"So when did she come back? How did she get in?" the police chief asked. He was still angry.

"I was at Lola's before the party. Ann was there," Rico explained. "She wanted to come here early. So I gave her my key to the house. I forgot to ask her for the key later on."

"Fool!"

"So she came back," Rico continued.

"After the party?"

"And she met someone. And that's who killed her, I think."

"You think!" said the police chief. "You never thought in your life." The chief was quiet for a minute. He looked into the fire. "Blade knows too much—about everything. And he'll talk. Rico—stop him talking. Now. For keeps."

"OK, boss," said Rico, "but there's another thing."

"What?"

"A reporter..."

"He's OK. I called his editor," said the chief. "I scared him."

"But he went to Lola's tonight," said Rico, "asking all sorts of questions. About Ann, about Blade."

The police chief went quiet. "Right," he said. "Then stop him talking too. For keeps."

CHAPTER
SIX

THURSDAY 8:00 A.M.

Nick slept in his car that night. It was too dangerous to go home. He thought about all the problems of the case. Why did Ann and Blade Raines leave together? Was it a drugs connection? Who met Ann after the party? Blade again? Was he the killer? And who was Doc Mansfield?

All these questions went around and around in Nick's mind. Finally, cold and tired, he went to sleep.

In the morning, Nick decided to find Blade Raines. He called someone at the newspaper office to get the actor's address. Actors always liked interviews.

Nick telephoned. "Hello, is that Blade Raines? I'm Nick Mason, from *The Herald*. I want to interview you, Mr. Raines. Today, if possible."

Blade said, "One moment." Nick heard another voice

—there was someone with the actor. Then Blade Raines spoke again. "That's perfect. Yes. Be here in half an hour."

Nick thought it was strange. *Why did he say, "That's perfect"? Who was with him? Is this a trap?* Nick asked himself.

When he arrived at Blade's apartment, the actor was waiting at the door. "It's good of you to come," he said. "Welcome to my little home."

Nick followed him in. It was not a 'little' home—it was large and very luxurious. And there were photos of Blade Raines everywhere.

Nick knew that Blade was an actor, so he did not believe the warm welcome. Was there someone else in the apartment?

"I want to talk to you about Ann Hammond," Nick began.

"Ah, yes," said Blade, "poor Bracelets."

"Why do you call her 'Bracelets'?"

"She wore bracelets all the time. To cover the scars on her wrists, you know. She was a lovely person," said Blade. "Do you smoke?" He offered Nick a cigarette. Nick fell into the trap.

As he took the cigarette, there was a terrible pain in the back of his head. He stood still for a second. Then he saw nothing but darkness.

Darkness and pain. Pain and darkness. *If I feel pain, I'm not dead*, thought Nick. His head felt terrible, but he was alive.

Very slowly, Nick opened his eyes. He was still in Blade's apartment. And there was a gun in his hand.

A gun! Why do I have a gun? he thought. He closed his eyes again.

When he opened his eyes again, the pain was still there. And the gun was still there. He moved his head slowly. Then he saw Blade Raines.

Blade was on the floor. Dead. Shot in the chest. And Nick had the gun in his hand. Suddenly he understood the trap. Now Nick was a wanted man—wanted for the murder of Blade Raines. The chief of police wanted to stop Blade Raines and Nick from talking. For keeps. This was his way of doing it. A very clever way.

Nick stood up quickly. *Get out of here. Take the gun*, he said to himself. *But not the front door. The back way.* He went onto the balcony and saw a fire escape. He heard the sound of police cars arriving, and he ran down the fire escape.

I'm a wanted man. The police know my car. Where can I go?

He walked away from the fire escape, into the crowds of people walking to work. Alone in the crowd, Nick had nowhere to go.

CHAPTER
SEVEN

THURSDAY 9:00 P.M.

Twelve hours later, Lola arrived at the club. When she went into her office, someone was already there. She stopped in surprise. Then she smiled at him.

"What are you doing here?" she asked.

"I had nowhere to go," said Nick. "So I came here. It was easy to break the window and come in." He smiled. "Sorry about the window. I also used your phone."

"No problem," said Lola. "But why here?"

"Blade is dead," Nick told her. "I know all about Rico and about the police chief. They killed him. But they put the gun that killed him in my hand. You can imagine what the police chief will do if he finds me."

"Blade too? Dead," Lola whispered. "First Ann, now Blade. Why, oh, why?"

"It's all one big organization. And they will kill

anybody. To save themselves. They'll kill me, and you too now, if they find us," Nick said.

"So *they* killed Ann," Lola said.

"I don't know," said Nick. "There's one man I want to find. Then I'll know."

"Please, Nick," Lola said, and came towards him, "be careful. You're the only one I can trust now."

She touched him. He turned to her. They moved slowly together and kissed. Nick wanted the kiss to go on forever. But Lola stopped it.

"You loved her. Ann," she said.

"It was ... a sort of love," he said. The memory was like pain—a pain that never goes away...

Flashback: March 1935, five years ago

Nick's memories of Ann were always of pain.

She always drank too much, she cried, she shouted.

"I can't live with her," he said, the last time. "I can't live without her." He went into the bedroom. She was crying again.

"All I want," Ann said to him, "is someone to love me. You don't love me, Nick. Not really. You don't want what I want." Her voice was strange, quiet. There was no hope in it.

"Stop drinking whisky, Ann. Then you'll feel better," he said. "See a doctor. He'll help you."

"I don't want to see a doctor. I just want you. I want you to say you love me. That's all. But you won't say it." She was crying again.

Nick thought for a moment. The answer was no. He didn't really love Ann. This was the end. He stood up and went to the door.

Ann came after him. "Please don't go. Don't leave me." She fell to his knees and tried to stop him from leaving. "If you leave me, I'll kill myself. I can't go on without you."

Nick stood at the door and looked down at her. He didn't know what to say or what to do. Will she try to kill herself again? *he thought.* Like before? *He saw the scars on her wrist.*

"I'm going, Ann," he said. It was the last time he saw her alive.

"Who is Doc Mansfield?" Nick asked Lola.

"Mansfield is a doctor," she said. "He gives Blade Raines the stuff."

"Stuff? What kind of stuff? Cocaine?"

"I don't know," Lola said. "Stuff."

"Do you know where he lives?"

"It's in the book on my desk," Lola told him.

Nick found the address. It was out of town, on the sea, at Zuma Beach. It was a place Nick knew. He and Ann went there a lot five years ago.

"Wait here. I need your car," he said to Lola. "But don't tell anyone where I'm going."

"I'll wait, Nick," Lola said. "I'll wait as long as you want me to."

CHAPTER

EIGHT

THURSDAY 10:30 P.M.

Nick took Lola's car to drive to Zuma Beach. He drove fast. He was angry now—angry for Ann. He wanted to kill someone; to have justice for Ann. But killing someone was not the way to do it.

When he arrived at Zuma Beach, Nick parked the car and walked down to the sea. He remembered walking here with Ann. Then he thought of his plan.

He took some seawater and splashed it on his hair, his face, and his shirt. He was now all wet and cold.

He went up to Doctor Mansfield's big house and rang the bell. He started to shake. But it was not from fear—it was all part of the plan.

A thin, old man came to the door. Nick remembered the lawyer's story about the men at the party: "a fat man, a thin man, an old man, and a very good-looking man."

Well, the fat man was Rico, the thin man was the police chief, and the good-looking man was Blade Raines. Was this the fourth man?

Nick was shaking all over. He kept to his plan.

"Doctor Mansfield?" he asked in a weak voice.

"Yes," said the old man. "What do you want at this time of night?"

"I need ... help. I need ... some stuff." Nick kept on. "Doctor, please ... It's two days ... I'm going to die." And he fell down at the doctor's feet.

The doctor quickly took Nick inside. The house was large and very luxurious. The doctor was a rich man. And Nick knew how he made his money. He sold drugs to people—people like Blade Raines and Rico.

The doctor helped Nick into his study. "How did you know to come to me?" he asked. "Who told you about me?"

"Blade," said Nick, still in a weak voice. "He said to come to you."

"It's very dangerous," Doctor Mansfield said. "Blade's a fool."

"*Was*, doctor," said Nick, in his real voice. "Blade *was* a fool. Now he is dead. And Ann Hammond. She's dead too. You knew her too."

"Who are you?" cried the doctor. With a quick movement, he opened his desk and started to pull out a gun. But Nick was even quicker. He took the doctor's arm and pushed the gun out of his hand.

The old man tried to fight, but Nick was much younger

24

and stronger. He lifted the doctor up by his jacket. He pushed him to the wall and threw him against it. The doctor fell to the floor.

"I spoke to the police today, doctor," Nick said. "Not to *your* friend, the chief. But to *my* friend in the police, Jack."

The doctor looked up at Nick. "I don't know what you're talking about," he said.

"I think you do, doctor," Nick went on. "I told Jack who killed Blade Raines. It wasn't me. It was Rico. Then Jack told me about Ann. The results of the laboratory tests showed she was a drug addict. Someone gave her those drugs. I think it was *you*."

The doctor said nothing.

"Start talking, doctor. Before I call the police."

The doctor began to tell Nick the story.

Ann worked at Lola's club. Rico was the real boss only the name was Lola's.

The doctor sold drugs to Rico, so sometimes the doctor went to the club. It was a safe place to go because the chief of police was part of the organization.

The doctor knew Ann. "A beautiful woman, but sad," he said. He spoke to her on the night of the party, Tuesday night, just two days ago.

Ann asked for help. She said she needed a doctor. She was a drug addict. She said Rico sold her the stuff. The doctor agreed to meet her after the party. "I wanted to help her," he said. "I felt sorry for her."

When they met later, it was about three o'clock in the morning. The doctor saw that it was a trap. Ann didn't want help—she wanted more drugs. But the doctor didn't have any drugs with him. He only wanted to help her.

This made Ann very angry. She pulled out a knife. She came at the doctor with the knife.

The doctor was scared. He tried to stop her. He took her arm and turned her around until the knife fell from her hand. Then he took the knife and tried to calm her. But Ann was still angry and violent. She tried to fight the doctor with her hands. In the confusion, they fell. Ann screamed. Then she was still. The doctor still had the knife in his hand—and it was in her back. She died in his arms.

The doctor was now in tears. "I wanted to help her," he said to Nick. "I didn't want her to die."

Nick phoned the police. "Jack, it's Nick," he said. "I'm at Zuma Beach. With an old man. And I know the truth about Ann Hammond..."

CHAPTER
NINE

FRIDAY 1:00 A.M.

"Why do I feel so bad?" Nick was drinking Scotch whisky. "I found the killer. Rico and the police chief are in jail. I saved you..."

"Yes, you saved me," said Lola.

"Justice for Ann. That's what I wanted," he said.

Lola touched his hand. "Like I told you—it's a big, bad world. There's not much justice in it."

"Ann was so lonely. So lost," Nick went on.

"Stop drinking, Nick. It doesn't help."

"Until yesterday, I was a good reporter. But this is a story I just don't want to write. It's too near to me. And now I'm just another drunk man in Lola's club."

"No, you're not. Stop feeling sorry for yourself," Lola told him.

"I'm going to tell you a secret," Nick said slowly. "I killed Ann Hammond."

"What?" Lola cried.

"We lived together. Six years ago," he said.

"I thought so," said Lola.

"And I left her. I just walked out and left her. That started her on the long road to her death."

Lola took Nick's hand. "Look, Nick," she said, "everybody dies one day."

"She tried to kill herself," Nick went on. "All those scars, those 'bracelets.' Because of me. The doctor put a knife in her back. But Lola—I put a knife in her heart."

After You Read

DISCUSSION QUESTIONS

Talk about these ideas with a partner or group, or just think about them.

1. Did you guess who the killer was before the end of the story? Why or why not?

2. Think about the main characters in this story. What were they like?

- Ann Hammond
- Lola
- Nick Mason
- Blade Raines

3. Describe Nick and Ann's relationship. What was good about it? What wasn't good? Why does Nick say that he killed Ann? Do you agree with him?

4. Ann was killed with a knife in her back. But the title of this story is *A Knife in the Heart*. Why?

5. Imagine it's five years after this story ends. What is Lola doing now? What is Nick doing now? Is he happy? Why or why not?

EXTENSION

If you enjoyed this story, see if you can find and watch some of these famous movies from this time period. You can watch them in your native language, or watch them in English with subtitles or captioned in your language.

- *Strangers on a Train*
- *The Lady Vanishes*
- *The Thin Man*
- *The Maltese Falcon*
- *Casablanca* (a little later in time period—1942 —but a classic movie with the atmosphere of those times)

Here are some authors who wrote popular detective stories in this time period. You can find translations in your own language, or challenge yourself to read them in English!

- John Dickson Carr
- Agatha Christie
- Ellery Queen
- Erle Stanley Gardner
- Marjorie Allingham
- Ngaio Marsh
- Philip Macdonald
- Dorothy Sayers
- Rex Stout

ABOUT THE PUBLISHER

Wayzgoose Press publishes a variety of books for both teachers and students of English, including self-study guides, textbooks, and more volumes in the *Great Stories* and the *Big Ideas* reader series. Find our full range of titles on our web page at

http://wayzgoosepress.com

To be notified about the release of new titles and special contests, events, and sales from Wayzgoose Press, please sign up for our mailing list (find the sign-up link on the website). We send email infrequently, and you can unsubscribe at any time.

www.ingramcontent.com/pod-product-compliance
Lightning Source LLC
Chambersburg PA
CBHW020346130626
46549CB00003B/1325

* 9 7 8 1 9 6 1 9 5 3 1 2 3 *